T0368468

Gingledorf

The Tiniest Fairy Moth of Them all

Written by

Marta Visola

Illustrations by

Avery Visola

AuthorHouse™
1663 Liberty Drive
Bloomington, IN 47403
www.authorhouse.com
Phone: 1 (800) 839-8640

Published by AuthorHouse: 09/25/2015

ISBN: 978-1-5049-3295-0 (sc)
ISBN: 978-1-5049-3296-7 (e)

Library of Congress Control Number: 2015913654

Print information available on the last page.

This book is printed on acid-free paper.

authorHOUSE®

Table of Contents

And So It Begins

Once upon a time in a faraway land, there lived the tiniest fairy moth of them all. Her name was Gingledorf.

One morning, Gingledorf was off doing her favorite morning thing, smelling the flowers, when she decided to stop to sit on a rock to gather her thoughts. Sometimes, this was a hard thing to do, because fairy thoughts might get sprinkled with fairy dust and then just fly away.

Now, we should all remember that Gingledorf is a tiny creature who is small enough to hide in back of a daisy, or get lost under a big maple leaf.

Gingledorf was the child of the queen of the fairies and the king of the moths. She had about a thousand cousins of all sorts and sizes. Some of them were moths, some were fairies, and some were fairy moths. Gingledorf just happened to be the tiniest of them all. And, through no fault of her own, she was just bound to get into pickles and jams of all shapes and kinds.

Gingledorf was trying to figure out the very best way to make some new friends. Sometimes this was hard for her, because she was not very good at playing the games that other fairies played. On top of that, she was very shy. Summoning all her courage, she decided to try again this morning. With a big sigh, she stood up and skipped into the woods.

In the woods, the other fairy moths had gathered in a circle and were playing dodge nut. This was a version of dodge ball played with a shiny round filbert nut that bounced and jumped just right. Gingledorf wanted to play so much that she was all aquiver, glitter sprinkling on the ground in a shower all around her. She shyly stood to the side and waited to be noticed.

Finally, her cousin, Malicesandra, forty times removed on her mothers' side, said, with a sly look at the other fairies, "Come and join us, Gingledorf".

Gingledorf jumped up and down so hard that fairy dust shot out from her feet and landed on the nut. She frequently had this trouble with fairy dust and stamping her feet. "Oh no!" Gingledorf cried. The fairy dust caused the nut to float away in the air.

And So It Begins

Malicesandra shouted to the other fairies, "See, I told you she would mess up!" and laughed at Gingledorf. The other fairies flew away to catch the nut, while Gingledorf left in tears.

As Gingledorf sat under her favorite daisy crying softly to herself, she heard children's voices coming down the path. She got up to hide as fast as she could, but she stepped in some fresh, sticky banana slug slime that was on the path, and she got stuck. Another disaster! If the children saw her, her magic would disappear!

Fairies, especially fairy moths and, most especially, the tiniest of them all, could not be seen by humans. Gingledorf struggled to get free but only succeeded in getting her dress, one wing, and part of her hair stuck fast to the pavement. The children were getting closer and closer.

Just then, a voice said in amazement, "What in the world is that?" It was the voice of a little girl.

Gingledorf stopped crying and looked up into the warm brown eyes of what she thought must be a princess. She was very beautiful with curly brown hair, and she was looking right at Gingledorf. Gingledorf looked at her own fairy arms, legs and wings; she was still whole and had not disappeared. She was not sure if her magic still worked, but, then again, it had never worked all that well.

Behind the princess came three more children, all boys. They squatted down on the ground and gazed in astonishment at the little flailing creature before them, as, by now, Gingledorf had resumed her struggles to get unstuck.

"Why, it's a little fairy moth! It is just like the ones that Nana told stories about. Nana said that they lived in her woods." said the oldest boy. They were sure that the stories that Nana had told were made up, but here was the proof right in front of their eyes. The other two boys, twins, just stared.

The little girl told Gingledorf to just stop struggling for a minute while they thought of a solution. The children ran to the house for Q-Tips and water.

Lickety split, Gingledorf was free, thanks to her new friends. They carried Gingledorf back to the house. Gingledorf told them all about her morning and how Malicesandra had made fun of her.

And So It Begins

The children, who were all cousins, did not laugh at her size or her magic that always went wrong. She was very happy. Together the children made a plan, and the next day Gingledorf was ready to carry it out.

Back she went to the woods and to the other fairies. Malicesandra saw her coming and asked with a sneer on her face, "Ready to play dodge nut again?" Malicesandra looked at the other fairies and laughed.

The other fairies were not sure what to do; they did not want to hurt Gingledorf's feelings. But, Gingledorf went right up to Malicesandra and said, "I know that you do not mean to hurt my feelings, but you do. I forgive you, though, because you are my cousin forty times removed on my mother's side. I want to be your friend."

Malicesandra was very surprised and did not know what to say. Gingledorf went on to tell the other fairies that with the help of some new friends she had come up with a new game. It was called Catch the Nut.

With a sprinkle of fairy dust, the nut went flying all over the place. Soon the fairies were doing somersaults and back flips in the air, trying to catch it. They all, including Malicesandra, decided that it was the best fun ever,

After the game, Gingledorf went back to see the children. She was quite proud of herself and thanked them for the great idea. She shyly asked if she could give them special fairy names. She decided on Princess, of course, for the little girl, Butterpickle and Chango for the twins, and Liner for the oldest boy. The children were thrilled.

"One more thing," she asked, "can we have my favorite food to celebrate? It is hot chocolate with two marshmallows and a dollop of whipped cream." The children shouted all together, "YUM!"

And so it began- the friendship that would last a life time of adventures. The four children and Gingledorf made the very best team of them all.

A Crushing Blow

Once upon a time in a faraway land, there lived the tiniest fairy moth of them all. Her name was Gingledorf.

One morning, Gingledorf was off doing her favorite morning thing, smelling the flowers, and skipping down the path she bumped her toe on something and went sprawling flat on her face.

She gave a cry and looked down at her knees which were bleeding and her dress which was torn. She sat and rubbed her knees and wailed. Just then she heard a gasp of pain and some small sobs.

She looked around and saw the tiniest snail of all, crushed under her bottom. She immediately jumped to her feet in horror. Gingledorf knew that something very bad had happened, much worse than her knees or dress. The tiny snail had a crushed and broken shell, and some bubbling stuff was oozing out of it.

Immediately, Gingledorf dropped to her hurt knees, ignoring the pain. Her knees would heal. The snail would not. She had done this. It was all her fault for not looking where she was going. The children had told her over and over to be careful, but she always forgot. Now look what happened!

With one antennae reaching upwards and the other bent under him, the snail was in bad shape. Gingledorf reached out to try to help him, but the tiny snail trembled and shuddered. He was trying to be brave, but now the sun was starting to come up, and, in addition to his crushed shell, he was drying out.

Gingledorf fluttered and flittered all in a dither. What could she do to help? She quickly got a leaf and dragged it over. She put the leaf on top of the snail to make shade. Now what? She needed help and she needed it right now. She tried to tear her dress some more to make a bandage, but it would not fit. She cried, "Do not worry, my little friend. I will be right back with help!"

Off Gingledorf flew to the house where the children were playing Cat in the Hat. They looked up in shock to see Gingledorf bleeding and torn. The twins rushed for the Q-tips which were always at the ready for Gingledorf disasters.

A Crushing Blow

"No, it is not me this time!" Gingledorf cried. "I have done a horrible thing. I was running along, well skipping really, and was not looking where I was going. I fell down and crushed the tiniest snail of them all. He is smashed, broken, and drying out!"

Of course, the children were ready to come to the rescue. Butterpickle reminded them what had happened when he broke his arm and how he had a cast. Now his arm was as good as new. They gathered Band-Aids. Chango got some play dough which he thought might come in handy, and Princess got some water. The children put their fists into a circle and shouted, "Children to the rescue!"

By the time they got to the little snail, it was almost too late. Princess quickly gave him some water. Liner, oh so carefully, put play dough around his shell to make it whole again. The twins used the Q-tips to gently moisten the ground around him so that they could pick him up on the leaf.

Off they went to the house where they made him a special little bed in a box with nice moist lettuce leaves and sang songs to him. They told him stories to help him forget the pain. Soon his shell was healing. After a few days, it was whole again, except that the green play dough had joined with the shell, and he looked a bit odd for a tiny snail.

Now, it was time for Tiny Wee One, as they had learned was his name, to go back to the woods. Princess, who was a great party giver, arranged a fine going back to the woods party with a nice vegetable cake for Tiny Wee One. There was a lovely side of water to drink, and goodie bags with the best carrots and chopped apples. They wished him well and carried him to a tree that they thought would be a nice safe home for him. They promised to come back often with the moistest of lettuce leaves and finely chopped apples.

Tiny Wee One told Gingledorf that he forgave her for hurting him. He knew that she did not do it on purpose. She thanked him for being so understanding and sprinkled a little fairy dust on him for luck.

After the children got back to the house, they made Gingledorf's favorite hot chocolate with two marshmallows and a dollop of whipped cream. They raised their cups and clinked them together. "To Tiny Wee One!" they toasted as they looked out of the window.

Tiny Wee One floated past. "Whoops", said Gingledorf. "Maybe a bit too much fairy dust?"

Apple Sauced

Once upon a time in a faraway land, there lived the tiniest fairy moth of them all. Her name was Gingledorf.

One morning, Gingledorf was off doing her favorite morning thing, smelling the flowers. She had decided to go down to the apple tree and smell the flowers that were planted there. The children had planted a rose called "Hot Cocoa" just for her, and it was covered with big fragrant blossoms.

As Gingledorf bent over, she was knocked flat on her face. Kersplat. A big golden delicious apple had fallen from the tree, right on top of the poor little fairy moth.

The apple was big, soft, and gushy. Gingledorf was buried from head to toe in apple slushy, mushy sauce. She could not get up.

Tiny Wee One, who was nearby, saw the apple fall. In fact, it had just missed him. At first, he laughed to see Gingledorf under the apple, but soon it was clear that Gingledorf was in real trouble.

Tiny Wee One rushed over as fast as he could rush. Which as you might imagine, because he is a tiny snail, it was not very fast. But, as he was nearby it was fast enough. He tried to shove the apple, but it did not move.

Gingledorf cried, "Glub Blub!" Tiny Wee One knew this meant "Help, Help!" What to do? He made a quick decision and started to eat the apple as fast as he could. This, of course, was also not very fast. After a few minutes of frantic eating, Tiny Wee One had not gotten very far into the apple and he was very full.

Gingledorf cried again, "Blub Glub!!" Tiny Wee One knew that Gingledorf was in even deeper trouble. He needed to get the children fast. Unfortunately, as hard as he tried, he was too full to move. His tummy was full of apple and was getting really uncomfortable.

Just then, Beatrice Bee came flying past with her baskets of pollen tied to her knees. BZZZZ. She zoomed down to check out the situation. She tried to help by pushing on the apple. But, somehow the end result was that Beatrice got stuck as well. All she could do was buzz frantically.

Apple Sauced

Tiny Wee One was getting more and more uncomfortable by the minute. His tummy was really rumbling now. Snails do not usually fart, or if they do no one would probably notice, but that is what happened.

Tiny Wee One farted, a big golden-delicious-apple fart. The fart blew apple slush off of Gingledorf's left foot. Gingledorf stamped her tiny foot. Fairy dust flew up onto Beatrice who was still pushing and caused her to blast away from the apple. Before she could stop, Beatrice rocketed into Tiny Wee One. Some apple slush and snail slime mixed together, caught and stuck his green play dough shell to the pollen baskets on her legs, and off they went.

As they sailed past the children who had come to the garden to find Gingledorf, the children looked up in astonishment. It was an amazing sight. Turning jerky summersaults, head over heels, the little bee with the tiny snail hanging from her legs sailed past.

Princess, thinking quickly, reached up and caught them. Liner asked, "Um; is there anything the matter?" Butterpickle bent close and caught a whiff of Tiny Wee One. "Does it have something to do with apples?" he asked. Chango just said one word, "Gingledorf!"

After carefully separating the snail and the bee from each other and putting them down on some soft grass, the children headed towards the apple tree.

When they reached the apple tree, there was a little foot wiggling around in the air from inside of a big smashed and squishy apple. The children quickly lifted the apple off of Gingledorf. Fortunately, Gingledorf was unhurt – just a bit sticky. It was nothing that Q-Tips would not fix in a jiffy.

On the way back, they stopped to be sure that Tiny Wee One was okay. They offered to give him some of his favorite chopped apples as a reward. But, Tiny Wee One slowly drew his antennae back and curled up into his shell as far as his still fat little tummy would let him. "I guess that is a no," said Princess.

After Gingledorf was all cleaned up, the children sat down for a rousing game of Cat in the Hat and some hot chocolate with two marshmallows and a dollop of whipped cream.

They asked Gingledorf if she would like something to eat with the hot chocolate. "Sure," she said, "As long as it is not apple pie."

Chester Drawers

Once upon a time in a faraway land, there lived the tiniest fairy moth of them all. Her name was Gingledorf.

One morning, Gingledorf was off doing her favorite morning thing, smelling the flowers, when she heard a distant crashing and smashing that was getting closer and closer.

She stumbled back in alarm and sat down hard. Fortunately, she missed Tiny Wee One who had decided to nibble on the flowers at the same time that Gingledorf smelled them.

The crashing came closer and closer. Soon, there was a screech and a gigantic smash, and then all was quiet. About this time, the children came running out of the house where they had been playing Cat in the Hat. They had heard the noise too.

They stood in silence and listened. Even the birds were quiet. The wind had stopped blowing, and was holding its breath.

There came a low moan from deep in the woods. Gingledorf immediately jumped down the back of Liner's shirt and peaked out from under his collar. Tiny Wee One "jumped" on Chango's shoe and tried to crawl inside.

The moaning continued and now became a wailing noise with a kind of a scritch scratch behind it. Princess and Butterpickle bravely said, "Let's go see what it is!"

All in a group they went towards the sound, Gingledorf peeking out from the shirt collar, and Tiny Wee One clinging onto the shoe with all his snail slime strength.

As they rounded the corner, they saw a horrible sight ahead. A truck had come into the woods, and dumped a broken dresser under the big redwood tree.

The children's mouths made big "O's" as they saw the drawers open and close. That was the scritch scratch sound. The dresser was talking in soft moans.

The children had never heard a dresser talk and were astonished. They realized, though, that if a snail could talk, and they could have a fairy moth as a best friend, anything was possible.

Chester Drawers

The dresser explained that his name was Chester Drawers. He had been dumped in the woods when he got old and broken. He cried as he told them that he had once been the dresser in a little boy's bedroom. He had held the boys treasures, listened at night while the boy sang softly and talked aloud to his toys.

Chester had felt like he was part of the family. He opened one drawer to show where the boy had colored a wonderful picture on the bottom of the drawer. Chester had been very happy. He felt loved.

Until one day the father took Chester out into the woods and dumped him off the back of a truck. Chester did not understand this at all.

The boy had certainly pulled too hard on some of the drawers, the fronts were cracked, and Chester had a broken leg on the front as well as a big split down his side. Chester still felt useful. But, father did not think so and had unceremoniously dumped him in the woods.

As Chester cried, the children and Gingledorf did too. Chester just wanted to be useful and be loved again. Gingledorf noticed that Tiny Wee One was not crying. He was just looking thoughtful.

Tiny Wee One had a plan. Before long, it was decided that Chester would be the home for all the woods folks.

Gingledorf got the top drawer. Tiny Wee One wanted to sleep under the leg. There would be a special place for all of the friends. It was perfect. Chester beamed with pride. He was needed, he was loved, and he was useful again.

The children got bright paint and painted flowers on Chester with names on each drawer of who lived in it. They gathered old soft socks for beds. Soon it was a wonderful place to live.

As the woods folks gathered just outside of Chester for a party and a celebration, there was much singing and laughter.

The children brought wonderful treats for everyone. There were grated carrots, crisp apples all in small chunks and, of course, hot chocolate with two marshmallows and a dollop of whipped cream. They raised their cups in toast to Chester Drawers and home sweet home.

Blown Away

Once upon a time in a faraway land, there lived the tiniest fairy moth of them all. Her name was Gingledorf.

One day, Gingledorf was off doing her favorite morning thing, smelling the flowers. As she walked along, Tiny Wee One crawled beside her. The tiny snail was telling about the yummy lettuce leaves that the children had brought him just yesterday, and how much he hoped to get an apple soon. Suddenly, a gust of wind grabbed the hem of Gingledorf's fairy dress and tossed it over her head.

Tiny Wee One laughed at Gingledorf in delight. "Why," he exclaimed, "you have on Wednesday panties and today is Friday!"

Gingledorf was a bit embarrassed, because she always had a slight problem with the days of the week, and that is why she had the special panties with days of the week on them.

In fairy school, the teacher had encouraged the fairies that had trouble remembering days, to wear these panties. Gingledorf explained that perhaps it was Friday, but Wednesday had gone by so fast that maybe it might be still Wednesday, and Friday was going to come in a few days – maybe next week. Monday was just a blur, Tuesday sounded a lot like Thursday, and so they did not count.

By now Tiny Wee One had stopped laughing and was looking at Gingledorf in amazement. It almost made sense the way she explained it.

They were so busy chatting about panties and the days of the week that they almost did not hear the sound of soft crying coming from behind them. The wind was still blowing, and, as they turned around, they saw blossoms from the tree overhead break apart and try to form again into the image of a little fairy.

The wind kept catching the blossoms every time they almost made the fairy shape. At this point, one leg was missing and so were both wings. There was part of a face – just enough to cry little blossom tears.

Blown Away

Gingledorf immediately rushed over. "Blossom!" she cried, for this was the name of the flower fairy that only had a shape in the spring when the blossoms fell from the tree. "Are you going to be okay?"

Flower fairies had a very short time every year to be visible and play with the other fairies, the rest of the year they slept and waited for the next spring.

Blossom told Gingledorf that she was not okay, and that part of her shape was missing and on the ground. The wind had blown her apart.

Gingledorf quickly gathered the blossoms and tried to put them back, but they just fell to the ground again. She tried to stamp her foot and sprinkle the blossoms with fairy dust, but they only started to fly away. It took quick thinking to gather the floating blossoms and put them safely under a little leaf.

"What will we do, Tiny Wee One?" cried Gingledorf with concern.

Tiny Wee One had an idea, but it would take team work. So Gingledorf set off for the house as fast as she could go, while Tiny Wee One headed in the other direction as fast as he could go.

When Gingledorf reached the house where the children were playing Cat in the Hat, they looked up at her flushed and flustered little face. As she came towards them, she tripped and fell flat. Her dress went up over her face again and her Wednesday on Friday panties showed.

Princess asked if the problem was that Gingledorf did not remember what day it was again. Liner wanted to know if she was hurt. Chango asked hopefully if she wanted hot chocolate. And Butterpickle started to look for the Q-Tips.

Gingledorf said that there was an emergency. The children did not even have to think about it. Their fists went into the middle of the circle, and they shouted, "Children to the rescue!" Off they dashed down the path to the apple trees.

When they got there, Tiny Wee One was calling in his loudest and best voice. "All banana slugs needed here, calling all banana slugs."

From every part of the woods, banana slugs were slowly crawling. They came from under logs, behind rocks and under leaves. It was quite a sight.

Blown Away

Tiny Wee One explained the plan. The slugs would crawl back and forth, over the blossoms. When the blossoms were nice and sticky, the children would put them back on Blossom.

The plan worked perfectly. Soon, Blossom was good as new, although a bit sticky and slimy.

Blossom was happy. Tiny Wee One was happy. Gingledorf was happy, and the slugs were very happy too. The children brought lettuce leaves and nicely chopped apples for the slugs and Tiny Wee One.

When they got back to the house, they all needed Q-Tips for a good clean up. And they toasted each other with hot chocolate with two marshmallows and a dollop of whipped cream.

Outside the window, the wind danced the flowers from the old apple tree. In the middle of them, somersaulting and cart wheeling, was Blossom.

It did not matter if it was Wednesday or Friday, it was a very, very good day.

Bees Knees

Once upon a time in a faraway land, there lived the tiniest fairy moth of them all. Her name was Gingledorf.

One morning, Gingledorf was off doing her favorite morning thing, smelling the flowers. As she bent over to get a big sniff, her nose touched something unexpected. It wiggled, jiggled, and tickled her nose which immediately turned yellow.

Gingledorf stepped back quickly and wiped her nose. Unfortunately, she wiped her nose on the hem of her dress which also turned yellow. She looked at her dress and then at the flower which was still jiggling and wiggling.

Gingledorf spread the pedals of the flower and looked inside. Struggling to fly was a little bee. This bee had bright yellow baskets of pollen attached to its knees, and the baskets were so heavy that the little bee could not fly away.

The bee explained to Gingledorf that her name was Beatrice Bee, and she was stuck in the flower. Beatrice wanted to make all the other bees like her, since she was the littlest one, by gathering the most pollen to make the yummy honey. It had taken her so long though that poor Beatrice had been left behind while the rest of the bees returned to the hive.

Gingledorf almost went to the house to get the children to help but decided to help Beatrice all on her own. The children would be so proud of her!

Carefully, Gingledorf put the bee on her head, draping the baskets over her ears, and started towards the woods where the honey hive was located.

On the way, she passed Malicesandra who laughed and pointed at Gingledorf. "Funny hat!" Malicesandra shouted sarcastically.

Gingledorf kept on walking carefully towards the woods with Malicesandra laughing right in back of her. When she got to the woods, Gingledorf carefully took Beatrice off of her head and set the little bee down on the ground.

"Fly up to the hive now, Beatrice," Gingledorf said.

Bees Knees

Beatrice tried and tried but could not get off of the ground. She kept falling back into the flowers that were very full of pollen. Soon she was covered head to toe in yellow pollen. This made her even heavier.

Malicesandra laughed more and more. Gingledorf was getting frustrated with Malicesandra, and we all know what that means.

Before she could think about what she was doing, Gingledorf turned to Malicesandra and stamped her foot. She told Malicesandra to just go away if she was not going to help, and to stop being so mean to her friend Beatrice. Fairy dust flew everywhere.

Some of the fairy dust landed on Beatrice who soared quickly up to the hive and crashed into it. Fairy dust sprinkled on the hive. The hive started to rise up in the air but could not go very far since it was attached to the tree.

The flowers that had been around Beatrice and were full of pollen now were full of fairy dust too. The pollen floated up to the hive in back of Beatrice. All of the bees came out of the hive and looked at the pollen. They started to clap and cheer for Beatrice who had brought back so much pollen and had saved them so much time. Beatrice was very proud and happy.

To reward Gingledorf, Beatrice asked if she would like some honey. Gingledorf was excited. She had never had honey. Just then, the hive stopped floating and bounced back into place. A little piece of the honey comb fell out of the hive and landed with a big sticky splat on Malicesandra who fell against Gingledorf. The two of them landed on the ground in a puddle of honey from the hive.

Gingledorf called up to Beatrice that she did not need any more honey but thanks anyway.

Gingledorf and Malicesandra were stuck together, wings stuck to wings, and dresses stuck to dresses. Hair and antennae were even stuck from one fairy to the next.

After Gingledorf got unstuck, Malicesandra said that she was sorry that she had been mean. It was hard for Malicesandra to be a good fairy, but she was trying, she said. Gingledorf said that she forgave her and hugged her. Of course, this led to getting stuck and then getting unstuck all over again.

Bees Knees

Gingledorf headed for the house with her dress covered with mud and dirt that was stuck to the honey. Her hair had leaves stuck to the honey that was stuck to her hair. In other words, Gingledorf looked like she usually did after one of her adventures.

When the children saw her, they were not surprised. They immediately got the Q-Tips out and started to clean her up. She was just in time, they said. They had a real treat for her.

They had some bread with some wonderful honey to go with the hot chocolate with two marshmallows and a dollop of whipped cream. They looked at each other in surprise when Gingledorf just started to laugh.

Building Lego

Once upon a time in a faraway land, there lived the tiniest fairy moth of them all. Her name was Gingledorf.

One morning, Gingledorf was off doing her favorite morning thing, smelling the flowers. It was a bright and cheerful day. Beatrice was buzzing happily. Tiny Wee One had found a nice moist area to visit with some of his banana slug friends. Malicesandra had even come down to sit by the pond and seemed downright pleasant. What could go wrong on such a beautiful day, Gingledorf thought as she bent to take a gigantic sniff of the orange tulip which was bobbing gently in the breeze?

The flower stared bobbing a bit more frantically and Gingledorf noticed for the first time that there was really no breeze at all. Oh oh, she thought and looked around for Beatrice. Beatrice was flying, with loaded pollen baskets, back up to the hive overhead. Nope, nothing wrong with Beatrice. The flower had stopped bobbing and Gingledorf sighed happily. Nothing wrong with any of her friends this morning! It was a perfectly beautiful day.

As she bent over the orange flower again, however, the day suddenly was not so perfect. Under the flower and twisted into a ball was a daddy long legs spider. Gingledorf jumped back in horror. Had she stepped on him! Had she hurt him?

She quickly got down on her knees and tried to straighten him out. She counted his legs. One, two three, four, five, six. She tried again. Still six. Daddy longlegs, as we all know have eight legs. The little spider tried to straighten his legs and look ferocious. He thought Gingledorf was going to try to eat him. He pulled his body up as high as he could and then collapsed in a tangled pile again. "Don't eat me!" he cried.

By now Beatrice, Tiny Wee One and Rocky had gathered around. At the sight of Rocky, the little spider stared shaking even harder. He tried to run away but he tangled his legs again.

Quickly, with reassurances all around, Rocky and Gingledorf said that the spider was safe with them and that Rocky was a vegetarian.

Building Lego

Lego, the little spider, had been having a horrible day. Well maybe he had been having a horrible bunch of days. Since he now only had six legs and used them to count, he was not sure anymore.

It seemed that the hawk had tried to carry him off and he had lost two legs. When he had tried to join the other spiders, they had called him names like Gimpy Limpy.

In fact, just then, Malicesandra came by to see what everyone was looking at and started to laugh at his six legs. She said that his name should be Legless, not Lego and she had never seen such a sight. She gave him a little kick as she passed and another of his legs fell off. Now he only had five.

The angry friends started after Malicesandra but Gingledorf said to stop. The most important thing now was to try to help Lego.

For this she said, they would need to get the children. Off to the house they went.

"Princess, quickly, emergency!" Gingledorf cried. Princess called Liner, Chango, and Butterpickle and off they went. They gathered up the little spider with great care and took him to the house. Lego was scared again, children sometimes smashed spiders, he had heard. Liner reassured him that they would never do such a thing and had even dedicated their powers to saving and protecting every creature in the woods. Butterpickle showed Lego how they stood in a circle and touched fists, shouting "children to the rescue!". Chango, in the meantime, had started to think of what to do. He was a master at taking things apart and putting them back together again.

Rubber bands looked a lot like spider legs, they decided. Soon, with some Super Glue and some slug slime, the rubber bands were attached to Lego's body. Outside they went. They told Lego to move his legs and walk. The rubber bands just hung there. They looked like legs but they did not move. Lego did not move. He just kind of listed to one side and flopped over.

Now it was Gingledorf's turn. She stepped importantly forward. She suggested that everyone step back and she would fix everything. She gently raised her foot and stamped a fairy stamp towards Lego. The legs sprung to life and off he went. He had more than a walk; he had a real bounce. He had more than a bounce; he had a jump. Even more than a jump, he had a leap. He soared over the flowers, over the bushes and over the trees. He leaped past the other spiders who looked on with their mouths hanging open. He leaped over Malicesandra who bumped into a rock and fell down. He passed the hive and Beatrice caught him and brought him back to the waiting children.

"Thank you," he said, "Thank you, thank you, and thank you so much!" Lego said that he had been afraid that he was going to starve to death since he could not catch flies anymore. The children had saved him and, thanks to Gingledorf, the other spiders would think that he was a super hero. "As my first super hero job, I have something to do," he said and back down the path he went to where Malicesandra sat with a cut and bleeding leg.

The children followed. Would Lego call her names? What would happen next? When Lego got to Malicesandra he looked at her cut and said that he could help. He spun some silk and made a bandage for the cut which quickly stopped bleeding. He said that he believed that if someone was mean to you, the only thing that you could do was to be double-nice back. He helped her to her feet and Malicesandra apologized for the name calling. She said that she was trying to be good but sometimes it just did not work out.

Lego looked over to the children who were discussing some kind of celebration. "Can Malicesandra be my guest?" he asked. Of course, the children agreed and there was hot chocolate with two marshmallows and a dollop of whipped cream for all. Not quite as good as a nice fresh fly, Lego decided but still tasty.

Spied Her

Once upon a time in a faraway land, there lived the tiniest fairy moth of them all. Her name was Gingledorf.

One morning, Gingledorf was off doing her favorite morning thing, smelling the flowers. Without warning, from on top of her favorite orange flower, a sudden SPROING caught her by surprise and sent her falling backwards onto her fairy bottom.

As she sat rubbing her behind and wondering what in the world had come shooting out of the flower in such a fashion, another sudden SPROING carried something through the air and over her head.

Gingledorf looked up quickly. With a little bounce and hop, her friend Lego came over to sit beside her. After a few false starts, since he was a little embarrassed, he asked for her advice.

There was a new spider in the neighborhood. The new spider was a little female spider and she had been looking all over for a perfect place to build a web.

Lego explained that she had 8 perfectly wonderful legs and the roundest of eyes that looked in all directions at once. In fact, Lego explained, she had eight eyes also. Gingledorf was amazed. Eight eyes! Lego went on to tell her that he did not think that he could capture the attention of all eight eyes and would settle for catching the attention of one. Could Gingledorf come up with a plan to help him?

With excitement Lego quivered beside her. SPROING! He jumped to his feet again, the rubber band legs working amazingly well. The new little spiders name was Lacy, Lego said. She was called Lacy since she spun such wonderful webs. The other spiders had been talking about how famous she was.

Gingledorf thought and thought. Was Lego falling in love?

Although Gingledorf had felt her own heart flutter a few times, she was no expert on what to do or how to do it. Her children would help.

Off to the house she went. Princess was the only one there and she was fast becoming an expert on dating. Soon a plan was set and put into action.

Sproing!

Spied Her

With help from Beatrice, a merry band of slugs and snails (Team Gastropod) and Gingledorf they were soon ready.

Gingledorf found a juicy fly and Beatrice coated it with honey to make it a sweet treat.

Team Gastropod crawled up and down the most inviting branch that was located right by Lego's new web. Gingledorf softly sprinkled fairy dust on it to make it glitter. Then they arranged flower petals in the slug slime which worked like glue.

In order to look as dashing as possible, new rubber band legs were attached to Lego - this time with rainbow stripes. Soon he was ready. With his fly held proudly in his two front legs he shyly started up the path to where Lacy sat with her back turned to him. She had just noticed the glitter branches and was staring at it in awe.

Gingledorf rushed to Lego. She whispered that she had forgotten to sprinkle fairy dust on the new legs and he was not ready to climb and jump yet. She decided to sprinkle a bit more on for good luck.

Whoops. SPROING! Lego shot up in the air and over Lacy's head. He started turning somersaults as he sailed past. The fly, carried in his outstretched arms dropped with a plop onto Lacy's head. She gave a little scream and stumbled forward into the slug slime and the glitter branch which bounced back, sprinkling Lacy with some fairy dust. As Lacy shot out from the branch with the fly on her head, Lego shot past in the other direction. They collided in midair, the fly now sticking them together with the honey. They fell to earth and landed on some soft grass while a merry team of slugs and snails, Beatrice, Gingledorf and Princess looked on with their mouths open in amazement.

After some untangling with Q-tips, introductions were made. Lego, with his head hung low, explained that he had just wanted to catch her eye. Lacy, laughing, told him that he certainly had. She said that he had also caught her back, head and legs. Lego, realizing that she was not angry looked up with a big smile. He invited her back to see the branch again and asked her if she would like to share the fly with him.

Of course, she agreed and off they went. The gastropods left for some moist lettuce leaves and Beatrice could hardly wait to get back to the hive to share the story.

As Gingledorf and Princess watched their friends leave, they had a great idea. How about hot chocolate with two marshmallows and a dollop of whipped cream? They would leave the honey fly treats to the two new spider friends.

Lacy in the Sky with Diamonds

Once upon a time in a faraway land, there lived the tiniest fairy moth of them all. Her name was Gingledorf.

One morning, Gingledorf was off doing her favorite morning thing, smelling the flowers. It had showered a nice spring shower and the flowers were glistening with drops of dew.

As Gingledorf glanced up, she saw something that took her breath away. Lacy's web which was right overhead and hanging between the apple tree branches, was covered with what appeared to be diamonds.

The diamonds had rainbow lights reflecting the morning sun and each one was perfectly round. It was amazing to behold. The light reflected from the diamonds was so bright that Gingledorf had to cover her eyes and peek out from between her fingers.

Tiny Wee One stopped in mid glide down the wet path. Beatrice stopped in midflight and settled on his back. Soon the woods friends were all gathered staring.

With a proud wave of one of her eight legs, Lacy approached the web. This was her moment and she was going to be sure that everyone saw her magnificent creation. Right behind her was Lego, proudly waving one of his rubber band legs.

When Lacy stepped onto the web something horrible happened. The crowd gasped a loud "NO!!!"

The web started to vibrate and when it did all the diamonds scattered onto the ground. It was clear that the diamonds were actually drops of water.

Lacy had worked on her web extra hard and it was her greatest masterpiece. The sun was shining brightly and there was not even one rain cloud in the sky. The diamonds were gone forever.

As they group of woods friends stared in silence, Butterpickle came down the path. After hearing what the problem was, he had a great idea and rushed to the house to get the others.

Lacy in the Sky with Diamonds

Soon they were back. Princess carried a couple of sequins. Liner had some shiny bits of flakes from his Liner rocks. Chango had some glittering threads and Butterpickle had some scraps of foil in several colors that he had left from wrapping presents.

After some whispered conversation, Tiny Wee One called in his most important voice. "Team Gastropod, report for duty." From under the leaves and behind the rocks, the banana slugs came. Soon each bit and bobble of glitter and shine was covered with slime. Beatrice carefully placed each piece on to the web.

It was wonderful, stupendous and magnificent. Such a sight had never been seen in the woods.

Lacy was proud but concerned. Orb-weavers, and Lacy was one, build a new web each day. Towards evening, orb-weavers eat the old web, rest for about an hour, and then spin a new web in the same place. Lacy had used up her energy and could not make a new web. The web was beautiful but it would no longer catch flies. Would she starve?

Butterpickle had another plan, and it was quickly put into place.

Over a picnic with fresh apples, grated carrots, and surrounded by many flowers, the friends enjoyed hot chocolate with two marshmallows and a dollop of whipped cream while they watched the web shine and sway. The sun made everything rainbow bright. Lacy happily munched on some flies that had died a natural death on the window sill of the house.

Gone With The Wind

Once upon a time in a faraway land, there lived the tiniest fairy moth of them all. Her name was Gingledorf.

One morning, Gingledorf was off doing her favorite morning thing, smelling the flowers. This morning she only gave a passing sniff and a kind pat to her favorite orange flower. Today was an important day, and she was in a hurry.

Down the path she went to join the other woods friends and the children who were sitting on blankets in the sunny meadow of the woods.

Up high in a huckleberry bush, and close to the fence, stood Lacy and Lego by what had to be a web that was two feet across. On the web, were many, many, and even more than many little baby spiders.

Lacy announced to the gathered friends that today was the big day and the baby spiders were going to venture forth into the world. She said that she had been a bit worried since they had gotten spring colds, but they seemed well now. This was followed by a few sneezes and some sniffs. Lacy glanced back with a worried look.

There were close to one hundred babies, give or take a baby or two.

The babies gathered on top of the fence in a row.

Lacy explained that the babies would make a balloon of silk from their spinnerets which were little holes on their bottoms, and float away to begin lives. She was sorry to see them go, as was Lego, but it was time.

The babies started one after the other to push silk threads out, and, for a time, it seemed to go well. Spider baby after spider baby took to the sky and floated out of view. It was amazing to see the babies carried on the breeze over the trees and through the meadow.

Left behind, with a few sneezes and sniffles, were two babies.

Gone With The Wind

When they started to spin their silk, it just dropped over their heads and stuck to the fence boards. Over and over they tried, until they were exhausted and now crying. This, of course, did not help the sneezing and sniffing.

Lego suggested that perhaps the spring colds had made their spinnerets not quite as silky smooth as their brothers and sisters.

What could be done?

Princess, who had been blowing some dandelion seeds and making wishes, knew at once what the answer was.

There was just enough silk that was sticky to attach to the dandelion seeds. Soon the babies were ready but there was no more morning breeze.

With that, Gingledorf stepped importantly forward.

She stamped her foot, and fairy dust glittered over the dandelion seeds, which shot up into the air, carrying babies dangling from them.

Higher and higher the babies went, startling the passengers in a passing airplane. Faster and further they went. Soon, they scattered far and wide. One ended in a bush on Meadow Grove Street in a back yard with an orange tree. One landed on Spring View Circle in a big bush. They were the glitteriest and finest spiders of them all.

As the friends sat with their hot chocolate with two marshmallows and a dollop of whipped cream, they wondered if they would ever see the two babies again. They agreed that it was possible that raising children might be a hard thing to do, but letting them go could even be harder still.

One Blind Mousie

Once upon a time in a faraway land, there lived the tiniest fairy moth of them all. Her name was Gingledorf.

One morning, Gingledorf was off doing her favorite morning thing, smelling the flowers. As she lifted up a pretty orange flower, she jumped back in surprise. Under the flower, there was a tiny grey mouse. The mouse had dirty fur, a torn ear, and his eyes were stuck closed. His tail was missing all the fur – and mouse tails do not have much to start with. Several whiskers were bent, and there were tufts of missing hair down his back. He shook and shivered under the flower.

When Gingledorf gently bent forward to look at him, he threw his little arms up in front of him and cried out, "No. No. Please don't eat me!"

Because his eyes were swollen shut and seemed to be stuck that way, he could not see the kind face full of concern looking down at him. He thought that it was a big hawk coming to eat him.

After some reassurances, and gentle stroking from Gingledorf he started to relax and told his story.

The hawk had come unexpectedly on his family while they were out for a stroll in the woods. The hawk had carried him away from his mother, father, brothers and sisters. It seemed to be miles and miles before the hawk dropped him in the flower garden where he had been hiding ever since.

Of course, Gingledorf immediately knew that she had to get help. After putting the flower back over the little grey mouse, she rushed for the house and her children.

She knew that Chango was the best child to help with this since he loved little mousies so much. Mousies were his favorite thing to draw and he talked about how wonderful they were all the time. He would be so thrilled to be the one to save the little grey mouse.

Chango, of course, rushed to help. Soon, the little mouse was clean and bandaged, and had a little peanut butter and some cheese to eat. His tummy was getting round and full and he was sleepy.

One Blind Mousie

What to do next? Mousie's family was nowhere to be found, and the little mouse needed to be outside in the woods where all mice love to play and scamper.

Fortunately, Chester Drawers had room for one more. Chango got a fresh sock that was soft and clean. Mousie was very excited. All the other folks who lived in the drawers said that they would help the little blind mouse.

Soon, Mousie was snuggled down in Chester Drawers. He had chewed the sock into little bits and made a perfect bed of them.

The peace did not last very long, however. The first time Mousie went out of his snug little home, the hawk, who had been looking all over for his dropped tasty tidbit, attacked.

With a screech and a gigantic flashing of wings, the hawk swooped down lower and lower. Mousie who could feel the shadow of the hawk coming over him, ran in circles, he could not find his drawer, and he bumped into a rock and fell down. He covered his head with his little arms and cried.

Beatrice Bee heard the cries, Malicesandra heard the cries, and Tiny Wee One heard the cries. Gingledorf, who was on the way to Chester Drawers to bring snacks to everyone, came as fast as she could.

Gingledorf stamped her foot and shouted for the hawk to go away. Fairy dust flew up to the bee hive. Tiny Wee One and his band of banana slugs, with quick thinking, threw slime into the fairy dust. Malicesandra gathered rocks and started to throw them at the hawk. Beatrice rushed to the hive to alert the other bees who tossed honey into the rising slime and fairy dust. The bees started to swarm after the fairy dust to attack the hawk, stingers at the ready.

The honey and slime struck the hawk who was swinging in wide circles, trying to avoid the rocks and bees. The hawk, with sticky wings, crashed into the trees over and over as he made his escape. Nuts and fruit fell to the ground in a shower.

Mousie, who had been in the middle of all the help, was hit on the head with a falling filbert. Everyone rushed to his side and looked down at the little mouse who was lying quietly on his back. In a few moments, Mousie shook his head, he could not see the faces looking down at him, but he could feel the love that they had for him. He got to his feet with help from all his new friends.

One Blind Mousie

It would be some time before Mousie could get around the woods without being able to see but he felt safe. The hawk was gone, and Mousie had a new family who loved him.

Gingledorf showed everyone the basket of goodies that Chango had sent for them. There were chopped apples, moist lettuce leaves, and cheese crackers. And, of course, Chango had included hot chocolate with two marshmallows and a dollop of whipped cream.

Gingledorf made sure that Mousie got the biggest cup.

Okie Dokie

Once upon a time in a faraway land, there lived the tiniest fairy moth of them all. Her name was Gingledorf.

One morning, Gingledorf was off doing her favorite morning thing, smelling the flowers. She had just gotten to the orange flower where she seemed to always find one disaster or another. She breathed a big sigh of relief when there were no hurt or frightened animals hiding under it.

As she turned away, her eye fell on a part of the flower that she had never seen before. It seemed to be fuzzy and twitching. She sighed a big sigh. What could it be now, she thought. She did not want any animals needing to be rescued today!

Of course, she quickly changed her mind when she saw the little orange stripped kitten whose tail had matched the flower so well. The kitten was looking away from Gingledorf and did not seem to hear her when she asked if he was okay. Gingledorf said "Ahem." in her loudest and politest fairy voice, but the kitten just kept watching Beatrice who was buzzing along, gathering pollen in her baskets. Gingledorf tried, "Pardon me.", "Excuse me." and a polite cough but got no reaction. The kitten just kept watching Beatrice.

Finally Gingledorf tapped the kitten on the shoulder. What happened next happened very quickly. The kitten jumped straight up in the air, and landed on Gingledorf. Gingledorf struggled to get free and got fairy dust all over the kitten. They floated up, crashed into Beatrice and landed on the ground in a heap at the feet of Butterpickle who had been walking down the path. Butterpickle helped Gingledorf separate from Beatrice who flew away unhurt. The kitten had not made a sound. He just looked from Gingledorf to Butterpickle in amazement.

The kitten could not hear and could not speak. Butterpickle said that this was called deaf mute and that there were many humans who were the same. The kitten had not heard Gingledorf calling him and so was very startled when she tapped him on the shoulder.

The kitten had gone to kitten school, however, and could read just fine. Butterpickle got some sidewalk chalk and soon they were writing messages back and forth. Before long, the sidewalk was covered in blue, green and red chalk.

Okie Dokie

The kitten, whose name was Okie Dokie, was on a great journey and looking for a new home. It was decided that Okie Dokie could move in with the other friends in Chester Drawers.

Butterpickle told Gingledorf that he was very proud of her for using such good manners and for not getting one bit dirty on her morning adventure. Gingledorf was very pleased to hear this and turned a pretty shade of fairy pink. She turned shyly around, blushing.

She asked if this meant that they could have a party for Okie Dokie. Parties were the best thing in the world! Butterpickle said of course, and they headed for the house to get the refreshments.

Butterpickle let Gingledorf carry the marshmallows down to Chester Drawers which she did very proudly and did not trip even one time. When they got the party set up with food for all and hot chocolate with two marshmallows and a dollop whipped cream for both Okie Dokie and Gingledorf, Butterpickle let Gingledorf add the marshmallows to the cups.

In went the marshmallows with a nice splash; out went the hot chocolate with a not so nice splash all over Gingledorf who was covered from head to foot. Butterpickle shook his head and got the Q Tips out.

They looked over at Okie Dokie who was shaking with silent laughter. He had decided that his great journey had ended in the perfect place to call home.

Love Is Blind or The Kiss

Once upon a time in a faraway land, there lived the tiniest fairy moth of them all. Her name was Gingledorf.

One morning, Gingledorf was off doing her favorite morning thing, smelling the flowers. Mousie who had been standing quietly on the path behind her sighed.

Gingledorf had been expecting something to happen that would need her help and so was not surprised or startled at all.

Mousie explained that he had come on a quest and could use just a little help. He told Gingledorf that he had heard that love was blind. He wondered that if love was blind and he was blind, was he meant to be finding love or maybe love was meant to be finding him. But, what was love? Why was it blind?

Gingledorf scratched her fairy head and sparkling fairy dust scattered over the flowers making them stand up straight and look quite beautiful.

Beatrice came by with her bee friends and thanked Gingledorf. "We just love it when the flowers are sparkling and so pretty," they said.

Mousie perked his ears up at hearing this. Love was floating around someplace. He just knew it.

After some moments of thought, Gingledorf knew that she needed her children to help.

Holding onto Mousie's ear to guide him, Gingledorf headed for the house.

With only a couple of missed steps and Mousie only crashing into one tree trunk, they soon were at the door.

The children were happy to see them and glad to help.

Out they went to the woods to sit under a tree in the warm sunshine and talk. The children explained that love sometimes found you in unexpected places and ways. If you were the kindest and nicest mouse or human that you could be, love would find you. They said that it could be like 4th of July fireworks when it happened. Just be patient.

Love Is Blind or The Kiss

As they walked towards the woods, a dark shadow crossed over the sun. The children looked up and Mousie cringed. He felt the change come over them and knew that it was trouble.

The hawk glided overhead carrying something in its beak.

The something was struggling and trying to get free.

Mousie yelled at the hawk.

Mousie jumped up and down and waved a stick.

Mousie tried to roar like a lion.

Liner ran quickly to catch the little something when it broke free from the hawk and plunged to earth. Princess, Chango and Butterpickle gathered quickly around.

Princess said, "Oh my, a little pink and white mouse!" And sure enough with torn, missing fur and covered with mud it was a tiny mouse.

Although Mousie could not see, he could hear the little mouse crying in fear and pain. He rushed to try to help.

Liner put the little mouse whose name was Pinky, gently down by Mousie. Mousie felt all over her body, checking for injuries. Fortunately, the cuts were not deep and would soon heal. Chango got Q-Tips, Butterpickle got ointment, and Princess bandaged her up.

Pinky gratefully gave Mousie a kiss.

Mousie, surprised stepped backwards and fell over Liner's foot, hitting his head on Chango's shoe.

In his head, he saw stars. Was this it? Was this the 4th of July fireworks? Was this love? He sadly turned away.

What could such a beautiful pink and white mouse see in him? He was blind. He whispered to Princess that he was going to go away now and could she please take care of Pinky.

Pinky watched Mousie trudge away, bump into a rock, trip and get up only to get tangled in some of Lego's leftover web. She rushed to his side and took his paw.

Love Is Blind or The Kiss

"Please let me help you, my hero," she said. "You saved my life. Even though you are blind, you still could see what needed to be done and you saved me!"

Hero? Mousie drew himself up straight and tall. He was pretty special after all.

A party was quickly made – a hero's party and a welcome party as well. There was cheese and, of course, hot chocolate with two marshmallows and a dollop of whipped cream.

Pinky kissed the side of Mousie's whiskers that had some whipped cream drops. Again, Mousie saw stars, and this time he had not hit his head.

Love? He could hardly wait to be patient and find out.

The Seeing Eye

Once upon a time in a faraway land, there lived the tiniest fairy moth of them all. Her name was Gingledorf.

One morning Gingledorf was off doing her favorite morning thing, smelling the flowers. She was doing thoughtful flower sniffing and hoping that she would get a bright idea.

Mousie, who was blind, now had a lot of confidence in his ability to get around the woods. But he was always getting stuck in one corner or another. Gingledorf knew that she must come up with a solution.

Tiny Wee One, who was looking for some moist leaves to eat and slowly following Gingledorf around, was also thinking. Soon he had an idea and got very excited. He decided to try it out all on his own.

He would be a Seeing Eye Snail. The children, who had explained to them all about Guide Dogs for the Blind, or Seeing Eye Dogs, had put the idea into his head.

Tiny Wee One hooked up a leash to Mousie. Mousie said that he wanted to go to visit the apple tree and try to find a nice fallen apple to munch on. Tiny Wee One thought this was a great idea. Off they went.

It did not work out very well. Tiny Wee One, being a small snail, did not move very fast. After a half an hour, they had made it to the edge of the woods which was actually quite close to where they started. They sighed and decided to think of another idea.

Several of the friends wanted to help. They tried Beatrice with the leash, but Beatrice wanted to fly in the air, and Mousie could not follow.

Just then Okie Dokie, the deaf mute kitten, came out of a warm patch of sun where he had been sleeping and stretched a stretch. He could see Mousie but, of course, Mousie could not see him.

The Seeing Eye

Now we know that cats and mice do not often get along very well and that was just what Tiny Wee One and Beatrice were afraid of. They quickly tried to get in between Mousie and Okie Dokie. Okie Dokie walked around them and up to Mousie and gave him a lick.

Beatrice and Tiny Wee One did not know what to do. As it turned out, there was no need for worry. Okie Dokie was just cleaning Mousie up which kittens like to do.

As Tiny Wee One watched the two he got a great idea. Okie Dokie would be perfect for the Guide Cat. They made a harness out of some twine and Mousie climbed on Okie Dokie's back. They were ready to go. Now for the next problem. Mousie could not see, Okie Dokie could not hear or speak. How would they let Okie Dokie know where to go?

Gingledorf, who had arrived in time to see the wonderful harness and hear the plan, said that the children had a sign language book in the house and off she went to get it. They all tried to figure it out but it was decided that Lego, the spider would be the perfect one to tell Okie Dokie what to do. Lego hopped on Okie Dokie's head, Mousie was on Okie Dokie's back. "Where to?" Lego asked. Before long he was signing to Okie Dokie and off they went.

Soon they were at the house and the children were so glad to see them. Lego had signed hot chocolate with two marshmallows and a dollop of whipped cream. Okie Dokie knew just where to go.

Rocking Rocky Rocks

Once upon a time in a faraway land, there lived the tiniest fairy moth of them all. Her name was Gingledorf.

One morning, Gingledorf was off doing her favorite morning thing, smelling the flowers. She sniffed and sniffed all around the garden. It was spring, and there were many beautiful flowers to see and smell.

After quite a long time of sniffing, Gingledorf decided to take a break and sit on a nice rock in the sunshine to rest. Right by the orange flower was a rock that looked just about right and Gingledorf settled down.

Soon, Gingledorf drifted off to sleep in the warm sunshine. Sniffing each and every flower was hard work. As she slept, she dreamed that she was moving back and forth gently in the sun, almost like on a rocking horse.

She woke up with a start and looked around her. The orange flower was now across the garden, and she was by the blue ones. She jumped up in amazement and scratched her head.

She looked at the rock and it was the same rock, just in a different place. Hummm, she thought.

Gingledorf sat back down, and the rock started to rock back and forth again. Gingledorf jumped back up as fast as she could and looked at the rock. After a few minutes, the rock started to move again. Four little feet came out from the sides, a little pointy tail from the back, and a small head with two bright brown eyes popped out from the front. The rock was actually a little turtle.

Gingledorf started to laugh. She said that she thought that the turtle was a rock. The turtle said that, in fact, he was a rock. His name was Rocky. They both had a nice laugh about this.

Gingledorf said that she had not seen Rocky before, and he said that he was new in the woods. He had left the far away woods and was looking for a new home. He said that the other turtles had made fun of him and hurt his feelings.

Rocking Rocky Rocks

Immediately, Gingledorf wanted to know why. Rocky turned his head and showed her the other side of his face which was one long scar. There were also scratches and little holes all over his shell.

He said that a hawk had tried to eat him and left a claw mark on his face and marks on his back before he could pull his head into his shell. The other turtles had called him scar face. Gingledorf told him that the scar was not ugly at all but made him look kind of strong and handsome. Rocky was pleased to hear this.

Just then, Tiny Wee One came from behind one of the flowers to join the happy laughter and conversation. As soon as he saw Rocky, he froze and started to shake. He tried to crawl backwards as fast as he could while drawing quickly into his shell. "Help me, Gingledorf!" he cried. "I am going to get eaten!"

Box turtles, like Rocky, love to eat snails and worms. Rocky started towards Tiny Wee One. Tiny Wee One just froze where he was and quivered. When Rocky reached Tiny Wee One, he opened his mouth.

He did not eat Tiny Wee One. Instead, he told Tiny Wee One and Gingledorf the other reason that the turtles had made fun of him. He was a vegetarian.

Since he had allergies to many things, he only ate grated carrots, moist lettuce leaves, and finely chopped apples. He said that he was sorry that Tiny Wee One had been afraid of him. Since he had been so scared when he was almost eaten, he knew what it felt like.

Tiny Wee One was very glad to hear this and told Rocky that those things were, in fact, his favorite foods.

Soon Tiny Wee One and Rocky were becoming the best of friends. Tiny Wee One invited Rocky to visit him in Chester Drawers and even live there if he wanted.

They turned to see Liner coming down the path. He stopped when he saw the turtle. In Liner's hand was a book about how to care for turtles. Liner was very excited to see Rocky.

He told Rocky that he had never seen such a beautiful turtle. Rocky was very proud to be thought of as being beautiful and he stretched his neck up as high as it would go. Then he remembered his scar.

Rocking Rocky Rocks

He just knew that Liner would not think that he was beautiful anymore and he drew his head back into his shell. Liner said right away how he thought that the scar was really quite wonderful and that it gave Rocky a super hero kind of look.

Liner asked Rocky if he would like to live in a terrarium that was in his bedroom all ready to go. Rocky looked at Tiny Wee One who was disappointed. Liner noticed this and said that Tiny Wee One could visit often, and he would take Rocky to the woods to visit Tiny Wee One too.

Rocky was glad to hear this because he really wanted to live with Liner who seemed ready to love him so much.

Liner invited Tiny Wee One to come to the house with Gingledorf for a welcome to the terrarium party. Tiny Wee One and Rocky had moist lettuce leaves, grated carrots and chopped apple leaves until they were so full that it was hard for either of them to get into their shells.

They laughed and talked together for hours.

Liner and Gingledorf had hot chocolate with two marshmallows and a dollop of whipped cream and smiled as they toasted the two new best friends.

First Star I See Tonight

nce upon a time in a faraway land, there lived the tiniest fairy moth of them all. Her name was Gingledorf.

One morning, Gingledorf was off doing her favorite morning thing, smelling the flowers and thinking about a story that she wanted to tell her best friends. This was a story that had been passed down from her father, the king of the moths.

Gingledorf called to her friends from the woods, and they all came from Chester Drawers and gathered by the pond. Her children came from the house and gathered there too.

Once they were all settled, with the shade loving creatures in the moist shade and the sun loving creatures in the sun, Gingledorf stood up importantly on top of a tree stump. Her story went like this:

Once upon a time in a faraway land, there lived a moth by the name of Georgie. Georgie was a small brown moth and many times went unnoticed as the bright and colorful moths dashed from here to there.

Now, this was good and this was bad. The good part was that Georgie did not get eaten since she was not easily seen and could get out of most situations where other moths got stuck. The bad part was that Georgie often times got excluded from moth games and the flower feasts.

At this point, Gingledorf looked around to see if Malicesandra was hiding and listening. Malicesandra was, in fact, behind Gingledorf's favorite orange flower.

One day, Gingledorf continued, while the other moths were escaping from behind a screen door of the house where they had been trapped, Georgie was pushed aside. Now, this too was good and this was bad. The other moths had rushed out and were flower sampling, but Georgie was stuck. That was the bad part.

The good part was that she noticed a shining light squashed down at the bottom of the door frame. Georgie fluttered down to look. At the bottom of the door, was a fairy that had one wing wedged into the door jamb and was struggling to get free. Most of the fairy dust had come off of its wing, and it could no longer fly. The door opened again, and Georgie helped the fairy up and away from the door. Still the fairy could not fly.

First Star I See Tonight

With quick thinking, Georgie fluttered over the fairy and showered the hurt wing with brown moth dust. The fairy flew free, with Georgie's help, the next time that the door opened.

When they were outside, Georgie realized that the beautiful gold and emerald green fairy wings no longer matched and one was now dull brown with no shine or sparkle at all. Georgie was very ashamed of her brown moth dust and looked around at the other moths who were brightly colored and rushing happily from flower to flower in the sunshine. She hung her head.

When Emerald, the fairy who Georgie saved, noticed the little brown moth's distress, she immediately put her arms around her and comforted her. Emerald said that she was proud to wear the brown moth dust on her wing as a reminder of the moth who saved her. Emerald went on to say that she was granting Georgie one very special wish that she could use whenever she wanted.

As time went by, Georgie had many chances to use the wish. She could have wished for beautiful wings, she could have wished for unlimited flowers to sip, she could have wished to be bigger, but she never used her wish. When she had eggs that hatched into little caterpillars, she was tempted to use the wish to make them have happy and long lives. She decided, after careful thought that it would be the best for them if they would make their own way in the world, which they did. There were times that she could have used the wish to help the other moths. Instead, she reached out with love to help them one and all.

Georgie grew older, and as she did so, she gained the love and respect of all the other moths, and many of the other woods creatures who she helped out of pickles and jams. She was known as being a kind and helping moth with a generous and gentle spirit. The wish was kept in a special little pouch close to her heart.

Now moths do not live as long as fairies, and soon Georgie came to the end of her wonderful life with the wish still un-wished. At the end of Georgie's life, with all her friends gathered around, Emerald appeared. She told Georgie that she had been watching over her since that day when Georgie had saved her. Emerald still had one brown wing, which she proudly showed to all. This wing, she said, had carried her higher and stronger than the other wing would have. Georgie held her old friend's hand in pleasure at the thought.

Emerald said that the wish that was un-wished had grown in power over all these years with every act of loving kindness that Georgie had done. Emerald said that with Georgie's permission, she had a last gift to bestow. With that, the wish started to become brighter and brighter until it glowed forth from the little moth, taking Georgie up and up with its explosion of light. Soon the sky was sprinkled with stars, each of them glittering with a bit of brown moth dust and a lot of wish glitter.

From now onwards, Emerald said, moths would fly mostly at night so that they could see the stars. They would always remember Georgie that way and Georgie always would be looking down at them.

To this day, Gingledorf said, moths still fly at night, and sometimes come to tap on our windows to invite us to look out at the stars.

So you see, Gingledorf said, it is not important how we look on the outside or if we are dressed in the brightest clothes, it is the measure of our hearts that we are remembered by. Also, in the night, when the first stars come out, we can wish on them and our wishes, if we have a kind heart like Georgie's, might come true.

With that, Malicesandra who had been hiding behind the orange flower came out and gave Gingledorf a big hug and kiss.

The children and friends immediately made plans for a twilight picnic with, of course, hot chocolate with two marshmallows and a dollop of whipped cream.

Later that night, as they lay on their backs and made wishes, they were all whispering to Georgie who would never be forgotten. They listened closely and could feel the wind carrying Georgie's love back to them

About the Author

Marta is a nana who learned that the very best way to teach life lessons is through a story. Her grandchildren always wanted the same story over and over, so she started to write them down. It was a family joke that when the children got a bit loud and rolling around like a pile of puppies, she could whisper "Once upon a time in a far away land" and they would instantly be quiet and sitting at her feet ready for another story.

About the Illustrator

The illustrator is her granddaughter Avery Visola, who is fifteen and started illustrating Gingledorf stories seven years ago. Avery combines the childlike innocence of the stories with her talent for capturing the emotion of the facial expressions of the characters. She is the inspiration for the princess character in the stories.

Printed in the United States
By Bookmasters